I Don't Belong Here

A HIWAY BOOK

I Don't Belong Here

by

DOROTHY KAYSER FRENCH

THE WESTMINSTER PRESS

Philadelphia

BOOK DESIGN BY DOROTHY ALDEN SMITH

First edition

Published by The Westminster Press®
Philadelphia, Pennsylvania

PRINTED IN THE UNITED STATES OF AMERICA

9 8 7 6 5 4 3 2 1

Library of Congress Cataloging in Publication Data

French, Dorothy Kayser.
  I don't belong here.

  "A Hiway book."
  SUMMARY: Already dismayed at having to spend her
senior year with her grandmother in a small town far
from home, Mary is horrified to find her grandmother
greatly changed, old, and forgetful. Then the young
man she met at the bus depot offers her help and
friendship.
  [1. Old age—Fiction. 2. Grandmothers—Fiction]
I. Title.
PZ7.F8885Iad   [Fic]   79–26905
ISBN 0–664–32664–1

FOR MY FAMILY—

Paul, Esther, Louis, Danny, Nancy,
Laura, Brent, Jason, and Brian

I Don't Belong Here

A HIWAY BOOK

1

NOBODY met Mary.

She stood on the hot pavement while the bus roared away, a trail of fumes behind it.

The fumes tasted like metal and made her eyes smart.

No tears!

Where was Gram?

Mary didn't want to be in Lost Creek. She didn't want to spend her summer here, and then her whole senior year.

At this lonely moment on a Monday afternoon in June, she needed a hug from her grandmother. A hello hug.

Gram was a hard hugger, Mary remembered. A woman who did everything with gusto. Yes, Gram was a peppy lady and great fun.

But to spend a whole year with her? Mary's heart cried no. Somehow, somehow, she would get out of it. Somehow! She set her jaw.

A doubt entered her mind. Maybe Gram

didn't want her, either. Why was she late to meet the bus?

Of course, she might be waiting inside the bus depot.

Mary doubted it. Gram didn't wait on the edges. She plunged in where the action was.

So did Mary herself. The two of them were a lot alike, Mary had to admit. But Gram was old, so old, and Mary was sixteen.

She picked up her red suitcase.

The depot's side door was warped. It moaned when she forced it open.

No Gram. The only person inside was a young man behind the ticket window. He was tall, with a pleasant face. He must be about the same age as Johnny Bryan, the boyfriend Mary had left behind in California.

Pretending not to notice him, Mary made a show of looking at the furniture—benches and chairs of brown plastic, cracked open, oozing cotton.

Seedy, she thought. This whole town is seedy.

"Can I help you?"

The young man had a deep voice. Mary liked deep voices.

She said, "Sure you can help me. Give me a one-way ticket away from here."

He laughed. "You only just arrived."

"Oh, did I? I thought maybe I was having a

10

bad dream." She turned and marched to the window, her heels hitting the floor hard, so hard they hurt. It made a nice, angry beat.

Traffic poked along the street. Mary stared out, watching for Gram's old Dodge.

Soon the young man appeared beside her. He squirted blue liquid on the window, then rubbed with a rag. In spite of the hot day, he was wearing a long-sleeved shirt—very clean and very frayed at the cuffs.

"Now I can see out," Mary said, "but there's nothing to see."

"You don't like the view of Jake's Pawn Shop?"

"I don't like Lost Creek."

His voice went cold. "A lot of people get grumpy when they travel."

Grumpy! The nerve of him! She opened her mouth to sass back, then shut it. He was right. She had been acting like a brat.

She tried to explain. "It's been an awful day. Good-bys at the airport—my parents going one way and I another. We might not see each other for a year!"

She swallowed her hurt, then added crossly, "Besides, it's almost impossible to get here from Los Angeles. First a plane. Then a taxi to the bus depot. Then the bus to Lost Creek. Now Gram isn't even here to meet me."

11

"So that's what's bothering you."

"Nothing's bothering me!"

He carried away his rag and window cleaner. He busied himself behind the ticket counter.

Feeling shut out, Mary wandered around the depot. Why didn't Gram come?

Luggage and freight were stacked near the ticket counter. Every piece was tagged. Home in California, Mary had filled out the same kind of tags.

She went to the ticket window, glad for a reason to talk. "Maybe my grandmother picked up my luggage. Three new footlockers, bright red . . ."

"Nothing red this week."

"They were supposed to get here ahead of me. I'll die if I don't get into some jeans."

"That yellow dress looks nice on you."

"Thanks." She felt warm and happy for a minute. Then a figure passed the window. Mary caught her breath.

But it wasn't Gram.

Gloomily Mary guessed, "She went to the wrong depot."

"We have four buses a day. Two heading north. Two heading south." The young man grinned. "Lost Creek doesn't need two depots."

"Oh, this dumb town!" She fed coins to the wall phone and dialed Gram's number. Ring. Ring. Twenty-one times.

12

The young man stood by, as if wanting to help.

"Of course she can't answer," Mary told him. "She's on her way."

Her brave pose was an act. She knew. Gram wasn't coming.

2

TIME dragged.

Again Mary dialed her grandmother's number.

Again no answer.

Nobody wants me. Not Mom and Dad. Not Gram.

Mary was worried. She felt sorry for herself. But something worse bothered her. Coldness crept through her body. Old people die, don't they?

Would she be the one to discover Gram's body, in the big old house on Elm Street?

She went to the ticket window and surprised herself by saying, "I'm sort of scared."

"Of what?" The young man stapled papers.

"Of what I might find."

His eyes met hers. "She'll be all right. She's just had a flat tire, or run out of gas."

Yes, Gram did things like that. But too much time had passed. Car trouble would be fixed by

14

now, or Gram would have sent word.

Her fear made her lash out. "Lost Creek does have a cab? One broken-down cab, maybe? I've got to get to Gram's."

"Why not wait a little longer?" the young man asked. "I shut down the depot at five. If you wait, I'll drive you home."

Home? In Lost Creek? Oh, never, never!

But it was a relief to know he would be at her side when she looked for Gram. She can't be dead. There was pain in Mary's chest.

"I'm Ken Clayton," he said.

"Mary Glass."

They didn't speak again until they were walking to the parking lot. Ken warned, "My car's a relic from the Civil War."

"Pulled by a horse! Just right for this one-horse town."

Ken kicked at a crack in the sidewalk.

With a stab of guilt, Mary said, "You don't like my making jokes about this town, do you?"

"L.C. has been O.K. to me."

"L.C.?"

"Don't you call Los Angeles L.A.? Why not call Lost Creek L.C.?"

"Sure," Mary agreed. "Why not?"

They traded smiles.

By accident, their hands touched.

Mary's breath caught.

15

Ken's car, dented and rusted, was a faded blue except for the door on the passenger side. It was shiny green, without a scratch. It was also tied shut with wire.

"You have to slide in under the steering wheel," he told her.

She slid.

He got in, putting her suitcase between them. "Guided tour," he said, and drove slowly.

Downtown was the same as Mary remembered, except for a new Pizza Hut. Hunger sliced into her. "Wonder if Gram likes pizza?"

"Too spicy for old ladies."

"Gram's a modern old lady! She's got lots of bounce."

"Young for her age, huh?" His laugh was approving. "Your parents must be glad you've got somebody—somebody modern like that—to stay with."

"Ha!" She looked sideways at him. "Maybe it's the other way around. It's giving them peace of mind, Mom said, to have me staying with Gram because she's a widow now."

I don't want him thinking I need a baby-sitter.

He kept quiet.

She tried to explain. "Maybe I'm not really mad at Lost Creek. Maybe I'm just mad at being sent here. Four days ago, everything was normal. Then, wham! A guy got sick. A guy I don't even

16

know. And Dad has to take his place. Right away. It's an emergency."

She gulped, then wailed, "It's down in South America. At a jungle camp. And my folks won't take me along!"

Mom used to stay home with me when Dad had a foreign job. She could have stayed home this time, just until I finished high school with my class. The pain cut again.

"Does your father go overseas often?" Clearly, Ken was interested.

"Has to. He's a mining engineer." She paused, then added, "I wanted to stay in L.A. Or else go into the jungle with them."

"No high school in the jungle," Ken said with a grin.

Temper boiled hot inside Mary. "You sound like my parents! Next you'll be telling me about kidnappings. About foreigners held for ransom—"

"It happens," Ken said, his voice low. "It's war, in a way. A few Latin Americans don't want U.S. companies doing business down there."

"Kidnappings happen in Europe, too. That doesn't stop people from going to Europe." It was a good point, Mary knew.

Ken took his gaze off the road long enough to eye her. "How tall are you? Five feet one?"

"Five three!"

"Five feet three," he repeated. "Besides, you

17

don't weigh enough to swat a mosquito."

He made her so mad! She just wouldn't answer.

He went on, his voice calm, almost amused. "You don't look like the jungle type of girl. All those snakes. Mosquitoes that carry disease. Wild animals sneaking around on silent paws—"

"The next block is Gram's block," Mary said sharply.

Ken drove so slowly that the car bucked.

Gram's block looked the same as it always had. Memories rushed back, memories of good times. But always before, Mary's parents had been along. Always before, there had been a limit to the visit, a one-week or two-week limit.

I can't stay here a whole year! I can't!

She tortured herself with questions. Why hadn't her parents allowed her to stay in Los Angeles with Molly Fisher, her best friend? Why hadn't she gone out and landed a job in L.A.—the heck with finishing high school? Why hadn't she married Johnny Bryan? Why hadn't she raised enough hell to get taken along to South America?

"Which house?" Ken asked, startling her.

She jolted back to the present. "It's the three-story one. On the right. With the green roof."

"What an old-timer! Porch all around."

"Gram calls it the veranda."

Now they were close enough to see the peel-

18

ing trim, the weed-choked flower garden, the dying patches of lawn. Dismay squeezed Mary's lungs. Oh, Grandpa! Grandpa, you're really gone! Grandpa had kept things picture-neat around the place.

Mary battled tears.

"There's a car in the driveway," Ken said.

"Gram's Dodge. That means she's O.K., doesn't it?"

She watched her own doubt show on his face. He chewed his lip.

Setting the brake, he said, "I'll let you out." He dragged her suitcase with him.

She slid under the wheel and joined him in the street. They didn't speak or move. The silence was a spell Mary didn't want to break.

"Well, so long," he blurted.

"Please! Please stay till I . . . till I see if Gram is O.K." Her hands were shaky, and so was her voice.

He reached to shut off the car's motor.

3

THEY walked side by side up the path.

Ken stopped on the bottom step. "I'll wait here," he said.

"O.K."

What was ahead?

Mary forced her feet to climb the steps, to cross the porch. The squeaky swing still was there, hung by chains from the blue ceiling.

What memories that swing brought back!

But Mary wasn't thinking about past good times. She was too nervous about this moment. Her fear squeezed tight and hot, like an outgrown coat. Something was wrong.

Her hand felt heavy as she reached for the bell.

Its three-tone chimes echoed from inside the house.

Nothing is changed, she told herself, not believing it.

She waited.

Nothing happened.

She turned to check with Ken.

He made the O.K. sign. She felt a little better, knowing he was standing by.

Yet fear squeezed tighter.

Then she saw Gram through the window in the door.

Gram came into the hall with a slow, halting step.

That wasn't Gram's way to walk! Gram was a full-speed-ahead person.

The elderly woman plodded to the hall mirror and pulled a wig on her head.

But why? Gram's hair was O.K. A little thin, quite gray, but O.K.

Moving with uncertain steps, Gram opened the inner door.

"I don't need anything," she said. "I just got home from the post office."

Mary pulled at the screen door, but it was locked.

"Yes?" Gram questioned.

"I'm here," Mary said.

Gram peered back through milky eyes.

"The bus got in." Mary's jaw felt frozen. This meeting was going all wrong.

Gram's lips moved in a ghost of a smile. "Why, Betty Sue! I didn't know you at first."

Mary's nervous giggle ended in a sob. This was

funny, yet horribly sad. Betty Sue was Mary's mother. Betty Sue was Gram's own daughter.

"I'm Mary." Her voice was a croak.

Gram stared back.

Ken called from the bottom step. "Anything the matter?"

With a rush of family pride, Mary said, "Everything's fine." She looked hard at the confused old lady. "Open the door, Gram. I've come . . . I've come to spend the night."

But that's all, she promised herself. I don't belong here.

"All right, Betty Sue." Doubt was thick in Gram's voice.

"Well, open up," Mary ordered.

With shaking fingers, Gram lifted the hook. And another hook. And another.

All that security! Years ago, Gram hadn't locked any door.

Gripping the knob, holding the door ajar, Mary waited for Ken to bring her red suitcase. There was no chance to introduce him. Gram had scurried away.

Like a mouse, with great fear, Mary thought. She wished Ken would stay, just to bridge the first few minutes, but he already was halfway to his car.

Gram was standing in the center of the living room, looking puzzled. The room was the same, with its big, dark furniture and its upright piano with yellowed sheet music.

Mozart mostly, Mary remembered.

Mary walked to Gram and announced, "Well, I'm here!"

Her heart raced. She was ready for Gram's arms to lock around her in the hard, joyful hug that was Gram's specialty.

But Gram's arms locked tightly against each other, at her own waist, as if she suffered pain.

She's grown old, Mary realized. Just since Grandpa's funeral, she's grown old.

4

THEN Mary remembered that Gram hadn't been herself, even last year. But they had expected that. Grandpa's death had been sudden, and they all were shocked. A funeral was no time to laugh a lot and be jolly. When Gram had acted out of it, they blamed grief.

"Where do you want me to put my stuff?" Mary was hanging on to her red suitcase tightly, as if it were a helping hand.

"Oh, you need a bed." Gram stood still, as if she didn't know which way to turn. Then she moved toward the stairs.

Gone was her bounce, her zip, her energy. Gone was her warmth. Gone was her love that used to bubble to overflowing.

Tears scalded Mary's throat. She pleaded, "Don't go up with me. Just tell me which room."

But Gram plodded up the stairs.

It hurt to watch her climb.

"Do you have pain?" Mary asked in concern.

"Doesn't matter," Gram said. Perhaps she added, "Nothing matters," but Mary wasn't sure she heard the words.

Gram wandered along the upstairs hall, opening doors. The guest rooms had not been aired. The beds were stripped down to their mattresses.

She wasn't expecting me, Mary saw. But plans had been made in long-distance calls. Mary's mother had talked and talked with Gram.

Had Gram forgotten? Forgotten that Mary was supposed to live here a whole year? Such a thing was impossible to forget.

Mary passed Gram's room with its wall of framed pictures. There were photos of Mary there, dating back to babyhood. And photos of Mary's mother as a child. And the old-fashioned wedding portrait with Gram and Grandpa looking so stern and young. So very, very young.

Mary went on down the hall to the next room, a big one with its own bath. Here the bed was made up with green-striped sheets and a green blanket, a corner turned down invitingly.

It was not the bed Mary would have chosen. But Gram was ready for her, after all. Gram had remembered!

Mary put her suitcase beside the bed.

"You're in Fred's room," Gram accused.

"I know." Mary mourned Grandpa. To be surrounded by his things made her sad. Her voice pitched high as she asked, "Isn't this where you want me?"

"Well, but it's Fred's room. He snores, you know." Gram's fingers stretched toward Mary, pleading. They were bony and frail, and trembled like twigs in the wind.

Yet her voice was surprisingly strong. "I keep everything ready for Fred."

Horror cut through Mary. Fred was Grandpa's name, and Grandpa was dead. Gone a year.

Something terrible has happened to Gram. Her mind. Her mind was gone.

Gram smoothed the quilt that didn't need smoothing and fluffed the pillow that didn't need fluffing.

Mary wanted to run. Run and run, and never look back.

Gram was bobbing her head, smiling. For a moment, she almost looked happy.

Yes, she did look happy. Waiting. Just waiting.

So what difference does it make? Mary asked herself at last. If she pretends Grandpa is coming back, whom does it hurt?

Not me!

Oh, but it did hurt. The ache drilled deep.

She fought for understanding. Her body was cold with goose bumps. Ghosts seemed to brush against her.

"Any room is O.K., Gram." Any room except

Grandpa's. She went on. "Listen, why don't I use the room at the top of the stairs? Where are the sheets? I'm good at making beds."

Gram supplied the sheets, then went downstairs.

Mary was grateful. She needed space between herself and the old woman—the fretful and confused old woman who wasn't Gram anymore.

She didn't unpack her suitcase. What was the use? Tomorrow she would be on her way.

Away. Toward anywhere.

She couldn't stay here.

5

ON Tuesday morning, hunger woke Mary. Dinner the night before had been small, just corned beef hash from a can, with an egg on top.

Eggs were about the only food in Gram's refrigerator, and this worried Mary. Was Gram getting enough to eat? Was it safe for her to live alone?

Mary couldn't answer those questions. She couldn't rule on Gram's future. It was up to her parents to straighten things out.

What a mess of worms to drop in their laps! Mom would have to fly back from South America. Dad would have to go to the jungle camp alone.

It was upsetting and frightening in Lost Creek. Mary needed Mom. She felt like a hurt child looking for a soft lap and a healing kiss.

Yet she wasn't a child! She should be able to handle trouble all by herself.

But she couldn't cope with Gram. She didn't know how.

In her gray mood, the yellow dress seemed all wrong. Oh, why hadn't she packed jeans in her suitcase?

"Darn mixed-up bus," Mary muttered. The red footlockers should have reached Lost Creek before she did.

She studied herself in the old, clouded mirror. A good enough face, if you didn't mind high cheekbones and a hint of shadow under the eyes. A good enough skin, if you didn't mind a few zits once a month.

But the dress wasn't her style. She was a jeans-type girl.

Ken Clayton liked the dress.

She would see Ken again today when she checked on her luggage. Her heart picked up speed.

Maybe it wasn't bad luck, after all, that the footlockers were late.

Aw, forget Ken, she warned herself. Soon you'll be gone from Lost Creek.

She couldn't stay, could she? Gram didn't want her. Gram didn't even know her!

Hunger forced her downstairs.

The smell of coffee drifted out to greet her.

Gram was in the kitchen, in a plaid apron,

29

bustling about. She wasn't wearing the wig, so she looked more like herself.

"Well, good morning," she said. "Did you sleep well, Mary?"

Mary! This was the first time Gram hadn't called her Betty Sue.

In other ways, too, Gram seemed back to normal. Oh, her steps were slower. She seemed unsure as she measured flour for her famous biscuits, made from scratch.

As she worked, she chatted in her old way, with friendly happiness.

"Remember how I used to cook up a storm?" She sounded wistful. "Everything ready before you arrived. Meat already roasted. Casseroles ready for the oven."

Mary remembered. "So many vegetables and fruits, they kept tumbling out when we opened the refrigerator door."

"Wasn't that something?" Gram sighed. "Nowadays I eat from cans. Makes chewing easier. And I buy ahead. I don't like to shop anymore."

"I'll go to the store for you, Gram. Do you have a list?" Mary wasn't fond of corned beef hash.

"Oh, never mind. There's enough to eat around here."

Not for me, Mary thought.

Gram served fried eggs with the biscuits, but that was all, so Mary opened a can of peaches.

30

Gram said, "By the way, Betty Sue and your dad phoned last night. They wanted to check on you."

"Why didn't you call me?" Mary yelled her question, anger at the surface.

"You were asleep," Gram said.

Mary wailed, "I needed to talk with them." I needed to tell them about you.

But Gram was O.K. this morning. Had yesterday been a dream?

Gram said calmly, "Oh, I wouldn't wake you up, just for a phone call."

"From South America!" Mary protested.

"You had a hard day yesterday. You needed your sleep." Gram was sure she had done right.

6

MARY felt like a prisoner at the bottom of a well. She was swimming for her life. Her only handhold was a link with her parents. Now that was gone.

Would they phone again tonight? Or should she call them?

I don't know what to do. I don't know where to turn.

She thought of Ken. He had a level head. Why not hint that Gram wasn't exactly—well, normal. He could give her advice.

She said, "Listen, Gram, I'm going down to the depot. To pick up my footlockers."

"Yes." Gram was paying scant attention.

"Where are the car keys?"

Gram didn't answer.

"I need the car to bring home the footlockers," Mary pointed out.

Gram said, "Fred never lets anybody borrow the car."

"But Grandpa is—" Mary bit her tongue just in time. She wasn't going to be the one to tell Gram that her husband was dead. She thought Gram knew, anyway.

"I have my license," she said. "I'm a careful driver."

"You can take the bus," Gram said.

Mary knew about the bus in Lost Creek. It had quit running years ago. There weren't enough riders to support it. The town was too small, and most people drove their own cars.

"This dumb town," Mary hissed.

She walked downtown, leaving the dirty dishes on the table. She walked with her heels hitting the sidewalk hard.

It was a long hike, but she needed every step of it to sort her mixed-up feelings.

Had last night really happened? Had Gram acted—well, strange? Then why was she more or less normal this morning?

Now, at least, Gram knew Mary was Mary and not Betty Sue. Things were looking up. Besides, Mary was too old to go crying to her parents at every bump in the road.

Yet things were not right with Gram. Her safety might be at stake. Old folks did set accidental fires, didn't they? They fell and broke their hips.

For sure, Gram needed somebody to watch over her.

But I wasn't sent here to be a nurse. Gram was supposed to take care of me.

Mary entered the depot, still wondering how much to tell Ken about Gram.

Four people were sitting in the depot, waiting for the morning bus.

They eyed her. She knew they would listen to every word she said. She was a stranger in town and a news item.

This darn town!

Ken greeted her from his ticket window. "Glad you came in. I've been thinking about you. How are things going?"

She could feel four sets of eyes on the back of her neck. Family loyalty made her say, "All right."

"That's good," he said, but his eyes held questions.

She burst out, "Is the bus about due? Think my footlockers are aboard?"

"You can depend on the bus."

"You sound very official," she said.

"This is a good company to work for."

"You're going to work here forever?" Her words sounded stiff to her own ears.

Ken said, "Gosh, no. Just till I save enough money to move to the city."

"I knew it!" Mary told him. "I knew you weren't all that crazy about Lost Creek."

34

"Lost Creek is my home. Of course I'll come back."

"But why?" she cried. She knew the four other people were listening, but she couldn't help it. She wanted to know what made Ken Clayton tick.

Ken said, "I have to go to the city to learn my trade. Then, when I earn enough money for tools and a truck, I'm coming back here to set up a plumbing shop. I'm going to work out of my mother's house."

Don't waste yourself in Lost Creek! Mary's heart cried. Aloud, she tried to make a joke. "I can just see that! Bathtubs in the living room. Pipes in the bedroom."

He grinned. "Don't worry, the house is plenty big. It held eight kids. I'm the last one at home. It's just me and Mom now, and Mom's sort of sickly. Dad died six years ago."

Mary felt weepy. Never had she learned so much about a person in such a few words. It was clear that Ken wasn't getting money from home. More likely, he was helping his mother.

Oh, he must truly love his mother!

Plus, he was dutiful.

He would never understand why she had to get away from Gram, to live this one year of her life without burdens.

So she kept her troubles to herself.

7

"RING around the collar," Mary muttered. "I hate you, yellow dress!"

But she had nothing else to wear, so for the third morning in a row, she slid into the dress that once had been her favorite.

Ken Clayton likes it, she remembered.

Well, so what? Soon Ken would be only a memory, left behind, along with all the rest of Lost Creek. I've got to get away from here. I can't stay here. I can't!

She checked the mirror. Yes, she looked upset. There was a grim line to her lips, a shocked arch to her eyebrows. And great sadness in her blue eyes.

Gram used to have clear blue eyes like mine, Mary remembered. Now Gram's eyes were milky, as if age had put a gauze curtain on them.

The mirror showed Mary that her hair was a mess. Had she packed shampoo?

She dumped out her red suitcase on the bed.

36

The ratty but loved panda bear. Hair rollers. Her high school yearbook. An album with her friends' photographs. An autograph book they all had signed at her going-away party. A chain belt from Johnny Bryan.

There were face creams. Lipsticks. Perfume. An address book.

No shampoo. No jeans.

But there was one wrinkled scarf. She pulled it tightly around her head, knotting it at the nape of her neck. It was purple and didn't look too bad with the yellow dress.

Hunger sent her downstairs. She had been hungry ever since arriving at Gram's house. Gram had lost interest in food, and she no longer cooked regular meals.

Yesterday, coffee had sent up a morning welcome. Today Gram had made no breakfast. The dishes from yesterday's meals were still stacked in the sink. Mary didn't give them a second thought.

Back home in California, housekeeping chores got done as if by magic. Mom asked very little of Mary—only to make her bed and to keep her door shut on the clutter, litter, and muss.

"Keep clean enough so you won't get raided by the board of health," Mom urged often.

It was Mom who pushed Mary to make good grades, to join school clubs, to take ballet and disco and gymnastics and piano lessons.

"Your job is to grow up," Mom said many times. "You'll have plenty of years, later, for housework."

The threat of housework was one good reason Mary had laughed when Johnny Bryan wanted to get married. The whole idea of marriage was unreal. Let Johnny find somebody nearer his own age!

This morning Gram's kitchen smelled like the rest of the house—in need of airing.

Gram sat at the kitchen table with her hands locked in her lap. She lifted her head to peer at Mary. She seemed dazed and troubled.

She doesn't know me.

Mary felt as if her insides had turned to stone. She forced cheer into her voice. "How are you this morning, Gram?"

"Gram?" the old lady repeated.

"Are you O.K?" Mary wailed.

Gram's milky eyes focused beyond Mary. "Is Fred stirring about?" she asked. "He doesn't like cold biscuits."

She thinks Grandpa is coming to breakfast. She won't cook till she sees him.

Mary's own hunger was gone, but Gram was frail and needed to eat. Mary went to the refrigerator for milk, butter, and peaches left over from yesterday.

She spooned peaches into bowls for herself

38

and Gram, feeling shaky. What if Gram asked for a third bowl, for Grandpa?

Gram didn't.

The peaches, cold and sweet, slipped down Mary's throat.

Next time I'll cut her peaches, Mary planned, watching the old lady chase the slippery fruit around the bowl with her spoon.

When the last morsel of peach disappeared into Gram's mouth, Mary poured Rice Krispies into the same bowls, saving dishes. The cupboard was low on clean china.

A sweet-sour, sickly smell floated in the air as Mary poured milk from the paper carton into a pitcher.

"Milk's on the verge of spoiling." Quickly, before Gram could reply, Mary added, "I'll go to the store today, for sure. I'll buy milk and some more food—"

"I'll go with you." Suddenly Gram's voice was strong.

That I don't need.

Mary pleaded, "Oh, Gram, that's too much hassle. I've got all sorts of shopping to do. Girl things. You know."

"I can't let you go alone."

"Gram! I'm not a child!"

Mary fought on, but the battle was lost. Gram was determined.

39

She probably is bored, Mary thought. Lost Creek was a very boring town.

She planned aloud. "On the way home, we'll pick up my footlockers at the depot." And I'll see Ken.

She finished breakfast, eating her cereal dry to avoid the iffy milk. The bread was too stale even for toast, she decided.

As she left the table, she knew she should still be hungry, but she wasn't. Worry about Gram had killed her appetite.

Upstairs she put on makeup, then retied her scarf, knowing she would have gone shopping plain-faced and pony-tailed if Ken hadn't been in the picture.

She was ready.

Gram had changed from her bathrobe into a gray wool dress. Wool in summer? Ah, well, old folks were cold-blooded, weren't they?

"You look nice, Gram," Mary said.

Gram was sitting on the edge of her bed, the wall of family photographs behind her. With tears in her voice, she complained, "My shoes don't fit."

Then I can go shopping alone.

Ashamed of her quick, selfish thought, Mary said gently, "Maybe I can help." She knelt beside Gram.

Gram's right foot was in her left shoe. She was trying to jam her left foot into her right shoe.

"The salesman cheated me. He fit me wrong."
Gram spoke with a whine and a tremble, exactly
like a youngster who tried and failed to do a simple
chore. Mary had baby-sat enough to know the half-
angry, half-discouraged tone.

"Let me help." Mary switched the shoes, and
they fit exactly.

"You're a good girl," Gram praised.

Tears blurred Mary's sight. Gram was a good
and dear person, too. But what was the matter
with her? Why couldn't she tell left from right?
Why couldn't she remember tiny, everyday
things?

Why couldn't she remember Grandpa was
dead?

Mary acted matter-of-factly. "Where are the
car keys, Gram?"

The old lady opened a dresser drawer. Her
bony fingers gripped tightly a ring of keys.

Feeling her heart thump, Mary put out her
hand, as though she expected Gram to give her the
keys.

Come on! Come on!

But Gram said, "I'll drive. Fred wants me to.
He doesn't want strangers driving his car."

"I'm not a stranger. And Grandpa is d—"
Mary locked her teeth. She couldn't talk to Gram
about Grandpa's being dead.

41

8

MARY sat on the right side of the car and watched Gram jab and jab the key until, at last, it slid into the ignition.

There were grinding noises. Then the motor caught.

Gram turned her body to check Elm Street for traffic.

"That's what I learned in drivers' education," Mary told her. "It's not enough to just check the rearview mirror." She wanted Gram to know she was a careful driver, that she could be trusted with Gram's old Dodge.

"Coast is clear!" Gram announced.

The car zoomed backward, nipped a bit of grass beside the driveway, and shot into Elm Street.

Then Gram shifted gears. The Dodge jerked forward.

Mary groped for the seat belt. Clearly, this was a time to wear a seat belt.

Gram was leaning forward, staring straight ahead, as tense as a Grand Prix racer.

Her speed seemed like a racer's, too.

"We don't have to hurry, Gram." Mary's voice was thin.

Gram didn't slow.

She hugged the right side of her lane, much too close to parked cars.

Air locked inside Mary's lungs. She knew the car would crash.

By the time the car squealed into a parking spot, Mary felt exhausted, as if she had run the Grand Prix on foot. It hurt to breathe.

Inside the supermarket, Gram plodded past the fresh fruit display. Mary trailed behind her, pushing the cart.

She called ahead, "Gram, look at the beautiful fruit. Pretty as a—a patchwork quilt."

It was true. There were bright squares of apples, oranges, grapefruit, bananas . . .

Gram plodded on.

"Wait!" Mary pleaded. "Let's buy some fruit."

"Look at the prices!"

Gram's voice carried. Other shoppers turned to stare.

Mary wished she could dive under the oranges.

She studied Gram with the eyes of a stranger. Gram did look odd in her too-warm dress, with her

43

purse held tightly against her chest and her wig atilt.

"I buy fruit in cans," Gram announced loudly.

Mary grabbed Gram's elbow and steered her around the corner, past the cheese and butter and eggs.

They paused to put milk in the basket.

In a low voice, hoping Gram would answer in the same way, Mary asked, "Is canned fruit really cheaper than fresh?" She didn't know. Often she had run errands to the grocery store, but she never had compared one price with another. Mom did that for the family.

"Cans are easier," Gram explained.

Yes, easier. Canned foods were easier to prepare and easier to chew.

Gram knew exactly what she wanted: peas and beans and beets in cans, German potato salad in cans, tuna and Vienna sausage and corned beef hash in cans, peaches and pears in cans.

Mary pushed the cart to the meat counter. "Oh look, Gram, look at the steaks and roasts." Her mouth watered.

The fresh meat didn't interest Gram. She wandered on.

I wish I'd paid attention at home. I wish I knew how to cook meat. But Mom had done the cooking because Mary always was busy with the cheering squad and clubs and lessons.

Well, so I'll eat from cans along with Gram. I won't stay here in Lost Creek long enough for it to matter. Mary meant to cheer herself, but she felt only sadness.

Gram was in the check-out line, pushing forward, crowding the woman in front of her. Her purse still was clutched tightly against her chest.

"Help me watch the prices," she ordered. "These newfangled computers cheat people, you know. Old-fashioned cash registers were better."

Now Gram's voice was hushed, secretive. Mary was glad about that.

The computer totaled the bill.

"Mercy!" Gram stared at the machine.

"Pay, Gram," Mary prompted.

Gram rummaged in her purse for her billfold. The whole scene passed in slow motion. Behind them, the check-out line grew and grew.

Gram plunked out paper money, one bill at a time, until many green rectangles spread across the counter.

People in the line sighed, and shifted foot to foot.

Her cheeks hot, Mary said, "Gram, now you need seventy-seven cents more."

To Mary's dismay, Gram pushed the billfold back into her purse. Again she rummaged in slow motion until she came up with a leather coin purse. The labor of counting out money resumed.

Nickels were mistaken for quarters.

Mary reached to help, but Gram slapped her hand away.

At last eighty cents in coins were lined up on the counter.

"Close enough," Mary said.

Swiftly, the clerk scooped up the coins and bills, and returned three pennies to Gram.

"It's wrong," Gram complained.

She thinks I cheated her. Mary's body felt heavy with sadness.

The bag boy lifted the sacks of canned goods. "Which way?" he asked.

"Oh, Gram, I forgot my shampoo!" Mary told the bag boy where the old Dodge was parked, then darted back to the drug department. Shampoo. Rinse. Nail polish and remover. Hand lotion.

Now that I have duplicates, the footlockers will arrive for sure.

On her way to the check-out line, Mary passed a bin of frozen foods. On impulse she picked up a pint of peppermint ice cream. Old folks liked ice cream, didn't they? This was a treat for Gram.

The computer was a hungry mouth, gobbling much of Mary's money. Thank goodness for the traveler's checks zipped deep in her handbag.

Gram was in the car, waiting.

Mary walked boldly to the driver's side. "Scoot over, Gram. I brought my license. Let me drive, O.K.?" Oh, please! Oh, please!

Gram said firmly, "Fred wouldn't like it."

The words were a fist whammed into Mary's stomach. Breathing all wrong, she made her way slowly to the passenger seat.

She locked her seat belt and prayed.

9

AT the first corner, Gram ran a red light.

The driver with the right-of-way slammed on his brakes. He skidded to a stop a mere two feet from Mary's door.

She felt the blow, as if there had been a crash.

Gram stopped in the middle of the intersection, blocking traffic.

The other driver honked angrily.

Gram stayed where she was.

He shook his fist.

Smiling, cheery, she waved back.

"He wants you to go on, Gram," Mary said.

When Gram started up, the green light was with her.

The emergency over, Mary sank into the seat, tired to her bones. Mom and Dad didn't send me here to be killed. One thing's for sure. I'm not getting into a car with this madwoman again.

Madwoman! The word grew roots that twined

around Mary, choking her. Was that the problem? Was Gram—crazy?

No! Oh, no!

Yet something was the matter. At times Gram made complete sense. At other times she was mixed up and forgetful. Then, once again, she became clearheaded.

Clear and muddled, back and forth. Why? Oh, why? The question beat like a drum.

I can't handle it, Mary thought. I need help. I need my parents.

But she couldn't talk to them with Gram listening. It would be too cruel.

She would have to call from a pay phone.

The depot came into sight.

Gram skidded the Dodge into a parking spot, banging bumpers with the parked car ahead.

"Mercy!" she exclaimed. "He parked too close."

Mary laughed to keep from crying. Gram was something else.

But Mary wasn't going to ride with her, not ever again. Beginning now.

How to worm out of it?

The ice cream!

"Gram," Mary said. "I bought ice cream. Peppermint. For a treat. Will you take it straight home and put it away?"

"I'll wait for you," Gram offered.

49

"No! I mean—well, the ice cream will melt. Besides, I've got lots to do here." She was thinking about the phone call to South America.

"Lots to do? Oh, the young man from the depot." Gram sounded owl-wise.

Mary touched fingers to her cheeks. They were burning. How could Gram, so vague, catch this tiny detail? Gram had cast Ken only one brief glance Monday afternoon. She hadn't seemed to listen when Mary spoke of him.

Yet Gram knew Mary wanted to be with Ken. Alone with Ken.

Years of living had given Gram wisdom about people.

Mary tried again. "Put the ice cream away, but leave the canned goods in the car. They're heavy. I'll carry them indoors when I get home."

Home! The three-story house on Elm Street never, never would be home.

"I love ice cream, so you can count on me." Gram drove off.

That was easy! Usually Gram was stubborn, making up her mind and never budging.

I'm learning how to handle her, Mary thought. She stood at the curb and prayed for Gram as the Dodge weaved into the distance.

I've got to tell Mom and Dad she's too old to drive. I've got to tell them how forgetful she is, and how she barely cooks.

50

Tears blurred Mary's vision. She hated the role of villain. Gram was proud and independent, and she would resent meddling.

I would, too, she thought. Gram and I are very much alike.

She entered the depot, looking for her foot-lockers and for Ken Clayton at the same time.

He was at his ticket window, wearing another faded and frayed shirt. This one was outgrown—his shoulders stretched the fabric.

"Bus not in yet," he called to her.

Good! She could spend time here with Ken and not look as if she were chasing him.

The trouble was, she had an audience. Two women and a girl about four years old were sitting on the brown plastic furniture. They were watching her.

"I should sell tickets," she muttered. "Every stranger who shows up in Lost Creek is like a freak in a sideshow. I hate this town!"

"What did you say?" Ken asked.

She could not repeat. He was loyal to Lost Creek. But she had to say something! She grumbled, "It's hot in here. Why don't you turn on the air conditioner?"

A dusty, rusted unit hung over the door.

He followed her gaze. "It used to work. Well, I guess it did, once—"

"Get it fixed." How bossy she sounded! At this

51

moment she was angry only at herself, but she sounded angry at the world.

She was wrecking her chances with Ken, but she couldn't stop herself.

Luckily, he only grinned, and said, "We're being patriotic. Think of all the energy we're saving."

The roar of the bus saved her from having to answer.

The two women and the child rushed outdoors. Ken followed. Mary tagged along.

Less than forty-eight hours before, she had been on a bus pulling into Lost Creek, anxious to see Gram, ready for Gram's hug.

Gram had not hugged her yet.

And every hour in Lost Creek seemed like a year.

Outdoors, the wind was gusty. A cloud blocked the sun.

The two women clung tightly to the little girl's hands while she tried to pull free. Her face was aglow.

An elderly man stepped down from the bus.

"Grandpa!" The little girl broke away, to fling herself into his arms. Soon the women, too, were caught in his hug. All four chattered, happy tears in their eyes.

An ache drilled deep to Mary's heart. She used to be a part of happy scenes like that.

Why was Gram so different, now?

The driver and Ken began to unload cartons and suitcases from the belly of the bus. Mary leaned to peer inside. She saw nothing red and shiny.

"My footlockers!" she wailed to Ken.

Ken asked the driver. The driver said he had handled nothing red.

"That can't be!" She had counted on those footlockers—counted on them for jeans, sure, and for everything else she owned. But mostly she had counted on a change in her luck. A switch to the better.

She felt pinned to Lost Creek.

10

MARY tried the café near the depot.

"I need quarters and dimes and nickels for this twenty-dollar traveler's check," she told the waiter.

"Then how could I make change for my lunch bunch?" the waiter crabbed. He wiped his hands on the soiled apron tied around his heavy middle.

"Sorry I bothered you." Mary was glad to leave the café. It smelled of rancid cooking oil and cigar smoke.

She walked five blocks to the bank.

And five blocks back. She wanted to make her overseas call from the depot and no place else.

This is crazy, she told herself. I tried to hide Gram's problem from Ken. Now he'll overhear.

I want him to overhear! she realized. He had a good effect on her. He gave her courage to do the right thing.

She went straight to his ticket window. "I came to use your phone."

54

"Only pretty girls in yellow dresses are allowed," he said.

"Things are dull here between buses," he added.

She could not help saying, "Things are dull all over Lost Creek."

"Well, we don't have big-city hustle-bustle."

"I've noticed."

Some of the coins from the bank were in rolls. She struggled with a wrapper and broke a fingernail. "Darn!"

"Need a helping hand?" Ken ripped off the thick wrapper as if it were tissue.

Mary made piles of the coins on his counter.

"Looks like you're going to call Siberia," he said.

"Siberia's no farther, maybe. I'm going to call South America."

He cleared his throat. "You—you have problems?"

"Do I ever! I'm all torn up inside. I've got to report to my parents—I know that. But I feel so guilty because it will wreck their plans."

"Wreck their plans?"

"Dad will have to go upriver alone and live in camp alone for a while. And Mom will have to come here to Lost Creek, to do something about Gram."

"Your grandmother needs something? Something you can't do for her?"

How could Mary explain when she didn't understand anything herself? She said, "Something's wrong, but I don't know what."

Ken offered, "Maybe I can help."

"How I wish you could! But nobody can, I guess. It's Gram's mind. It comes and goes."

She poked at the piles of coins. "I'd better get with it."

There were too many coins to hold in one hand. She pulled off her purple scarf to make a pouch for the money.

"Don't look at my hair," she ordered.

"You always look nice."

Mary felt a glow that had nothing to do with the heat of the depot. How different Ken was from Johnny Bryan.

Johnny had kidded her with insults, calling her Bag of Bones and Cross-Eyed Zebra and Stupid Broad.

How could anybody feel romantic toward a guy who called her a stupid broad?

But if she had married Johnny, she wouldn't be here in Lost Creek, worried out of her wits about Gram.

Then nobody in the family would know Gram needed help.

"I'd better get with it," she said again. "Stir up a hornet's nest."

56

"Is it necessary?" Ken sounded doubtful.

"I don't know! But I don't want Gram killing herself in that car." The pouch of money was heavy.

Her fingers trembled when she fed a coin to the wall phone. Her voice sounded young and scared, even to her own ears.

"I want to place an overseas call, person-to-person." She told the operator her parents' name, the name of their hotel, and its phone number.

"Don't deposit the coins until I reach your party," the operator instructed.

Deposit the coins! How could she? She needed a third hand.

Squeezing the phone between her ear and her shoulder, she reached toward the pouch.

The phone slipped.

She grabbed for it.

As she grabbed, corners of the pouch came loose. Coins hit the floor like hail. They rolled everywhere.

"Help!" she yelled.

In moments Ken was on his hands and knees, reaching under furniture for stray coins, getting his jeans dusty. He brought Mary one handful of money, then hunted more.

Her breath caught in her lungs as she heard the phone answered so far away. The name of her parents' hotel sounded romantic, pronounced in a

Latin tongue. Oh, she could hear perfectly!

In English, Mary's operator asked for Mr. or Mrs. Glass.

Having heard English, the hotel operator responded in English. Mr. and Mrs. Glass had checked out.

"That can't be," Mary argued. "They will be there another day or two, at least."

The Lost Creek operator cut in. "Do you have another number to try?"

With new hope, Mary gave the number of the South American office of Dad's company. Surely that was where he and Mom would be, getting briefed on the problems of the jungle camp.

The company line was busy.

While Mary waited for her call-back, she paced the waiting room. She could not sit still. She could not even stand in one spot. She was like a toy with its spring wound too tight.

After five minutes of waiting and pacing, Mary began to tell Ken what she meant to tell her parents. Talking out loud helped her to think better.

She knew she could trust Ken not to blab secrets.

At last, the call-back came.

Mr. and Mrs. Glass had begun their trip upriver. The boat sailed only once a week, and the emergency at the jungle camp was serious.

The message fell on Mary like a hatchet.

She was too late.

11

THE shade snapped.

Mary jolted awake. Sunlight was strong in her room, but that didn't mean she had to get up, did it? This was summer vacation.

Besides, there was nothing to do in Lost Creek. Nothing—at least until the morning bus was due. Then she'd go pick up her footlockers. Oh, they had to come today!

She burrowed into her pillow, squeezing her eyes shut. She would sleep on. She would ignore the sun.

"Well, young lady," said a deep voice. "You haven't been much help around here, have you?"

That rasping voice! Mary would know it anywhere. Olga had been Gram's cleaning lady forever.

Mary sat up, sleep forgotten. "Olga! Is that you? Is that really you?"

The gritty voice answered, "It's Thursday, isn't it? Haven't missed a Thursday in thirty

60

years." Her chin jutted with pride.

Mary smiled a secret smile. Olga was loved. She was gruff, outspoken, and bossy. She even bossed Gram and got away with it. Maybe things would shift back to normal with her here.

Olga crossed slowly from the window toward Mary's bed, wincing at every step.

Mary's heart twisted. Olga was as old as Gram, and the years were telling on her, too. She was overweight and hurting with arthritis. Now her hair was solid silver.

"Your grandmother didn't tell me you were coming." Olga sounded angry, as though it were all Mary's fault.

Mary wailed, "She didn't tell you because she didn't remember! Mom phoned her a million times, about plans, but still she didn't remember. She didn't even meet my bus." That memory still hurt.

Olga's head wagged side to side. "She forgot you were coming, I suppose, the minute she hung up the telephone."

"That's not possible! How could she?"

Olga limped her way to the chair and lowered herself with a moan. "How could she?" she echoed. "Well, she's forgetful."

"Forgetful! You're telling me?" Mary's laugh had tears in it.

With effort, Olga bent over and rubbed her

61

ankles. "Folks change when they get old."

"Not you, Olga. You don't change."

"I've been lucky."

Lucky! Crippled and old, and still doing other people's housework. That was luck?

Olga straightened her body until she was sitting tall, and even that small effort winded her. Gasping, she stated, "I'm not a burden to anybody."

"Gram doesn't want to be a burden, either. I can see that. She wants to keep on doing everything she's always done. She won't let me drive."

"More's the pity," Olga said.

Joy jumped in Mary's heart. Olga is on my side.

The old woman said, "Be patient with your grandmother. She's not herself."

"Then who is she?" Mary yelled the question.

Olga's answer was no answer. "She lives a lot in the past."

"She remembers the past, that's for sure. Every detail of it. Then she forgets what happened yesterday." It felt good to pour out her heart to Olga.

Mary added, "Know what bugs me most? It's the way she pretends Grandpa is alive."

Olga nodded. "She has good days and bad days. Clear days and hazy days."

"She's not so hazy," Mary argued. "She knows

darn well that Grandpa is dead! I think she dreams him alive, just for company."

"Company she needs, all right. And that's up to you."

"Olga, you don't understand! I won't be around long." Not long after Mom and Dad receive the letter I'm going to write.

Olga said, "Don't lay that snooty tone on me, young lady. As long as you're here, you'd better be useful."

What am I supposed to do? The housework you're paid to do? Immediately Mary felt shame. She wasn't nasty by nature—especially not toward old ladies. She wasn't lazy.

The trouble was, she really didn't notice the messes she and Gram made. Dishes stacked up in the sink, sure, but home in California there was a dishwasher. Old newspapers piled up on the coffee table, but it wasn't Mary's job to throw them away.

Or was it?

The canned foods bought yesterday still were in sacks on the kitchen counter. Mary had meant to put them away, but the melted ice cream had jarred her off the track.

"Guess what happened yesterday, Olga?" Mary used her warpath voice. "I bought peppermint ice cream for Gram. I told her to put it away when she got home. I told her and told her. But she

63

didn't, so it melted to yuk, and we had to throw it down the sink."

"She forgets," Olga said.

They were going around in circles, always coming back to the fact that Gram forgot. But why did she forget? Mary needed a good reason. Or else she needed Gram to shape up.

"About forgetting," Olga went on, "I have a small job for you."

"Sure." Mary was willing to help, if only she knew how.

"Now here's what you do." Olga's rasping voice lowered to a gritty whisper. "After your grandmother is in bed at night, I want you to go into her room. Pick up her underwear. Put it in the wash."

"She'd be insulted."

"If you handle it right, she won't notice. Otherwise she wears the same underwear all week."

"Gross!"

The two stared at each other.

Mary said, "Gram used to smell like flowers."

"I remember," Olga said.

Mary rushed to Gram's defense. "She never smells dirty! She smells like—well, like musty books from the attic."

Olga sighed. "Likely, she's afraid the washing machine will wear things out. Or else she's trying to save soap and water. She's getting stingy."

64

"She really counts her money." Mary almost told about the embarrassments of shopping with Gram, but she kept quiet out of loyalty.

She made no promises about the underwear.

With effort, Olga heaved herself out of the chair. She walked with pain. At the door, she turned to face Mary.

"Well, I guess it's a good thing you're here." She sounded doubtful. "You and your grand-mother—you can take care of each other."

I can't take care of anybody! I don't know how!

All hope of sleeping was gone. Mary dressed and went downstairs.

Olga was vacuuming the living room, and Gram was nowhere in sight.

I guess I'll have to fix my own breakfast. That she could manage. But she didn't like to eat alone.

The kitchen was dismal. Three days' worth of dirty dishes still crowded the sink.

Mary shrugged. Olga would wash the dishes. It was her job.

But Olga was old and lame.

The work I do now, Mary figured, Olga won't have to do later.

She plugged the sink, poured soap, ran hot water. Suds foamed high.

Through her tears, every bubble made a rain-bow.

12

IT was late Friday morning.

"Good news," said the low voice on the phone.

Nothing more needed to be said.

Mary felt like dancing. "Oh, Ken, thanks for calling!"

He said, "One of your footlockers came in."

Her feet went heavy, too clumsy for dancing. "Just one? With my luck, it'll be one without jeans."

Her yellow dress looked awful because she had washed it in the bathroom sink. It was supposed to be drip-dry, but it looked like a waffle.

I'm going to bury this dress when I get into jeans—if I ever do.

Ken said, "Nothing wrong with your luck. I was teasing. All three footlockers came in this morning."

Thank goodness.

But now I won't have an excuse for hanging around the depot.

She said, "Listen, Ken, I planned to be down there this morning when the bus came in. But I couldn't leave Gram. She kept watching for Olga —that's the cleaning lady. Gram kept saying today was Olga's day. Ken—Olga was here yesterday."

"Don't let it get you down," he told her.

"Easy enough for you to say—"

Sharply he changed the subject. "I'll take good care of your luggage. The trouble is, it's pretty banged up. Dented and scratched."

"My tape player! My hair dryer! Ken, darn it, you said I could trust the bus."

He laughed. "Can't you tell when I'm kidding?"

"Everything's O.K?" she checked.

"Little scratches. Little dents. Just the normal wear and tear."

"I'd better check it out." Soon as I can leave Gram, I'll see Ken. Her heart was as light as a balloon.

He said, "Listen, I know you can't use your grandmother's car—"

Mary interrupted. "I ask her and ask her, but she won't give me the keys."

"Well, how's this for an idea? When I shut the depot at five, why don't I bring your footlockers?"

He wants to see me! He wants to talk with me, and not just to kill time during working hours. She danced a bit of disco.

"How does that suit you?" He sounded anxious.

"Well, that sounds all right." What an understatement! "I suppose it's part of the bus company service, to deliver late luggage?"

"There'll be a charge," he warned.

This time she caught the teasing. If the cost was a kiss, she would pay cheerfully.

The conversation ended.

Ken was coming over! It was almost a date! Still dancing disco, Mary joined Gram in the living room.

Compared with Mary, Gram was calm. She quit talking about Olga. Now Mary felt safe to leave her alone.

She took the shopping list and the ten dollars Gram gave her and hiked to the store.

Gram's list was short: bread, noodles, chicken-rice soup. For herself, from her own money, Mary bought a roll of mints—the kind that promised "kissing-sweet breath."

She felt wonderful.

As she neared the check-out line, she passed a display of plants. Each pot was wrapped in bright, glossy foil.

The flowers reminded Mary of the ones

Grandpa had grown in the yard. How Gram had loved to cut those garden flowers, to arrange them in vases, to place them all over the house!

I'll bet she'd like a plant!

Mary already knew the kind she would choose. Tiger lilies. They had personality! Their red-orange petals bent backward as if bragging, "Look, Ma, no cavities!" And the big, black spots on the petals were like freckles.

Mary debated. The more blooms, the higher the price. She wanted the best for Gram, but she had been spending too much money.

She decided on a pot with red foil, red ribbon, and three perky blooms.

She put it gently into her basket. "Gram will love you."

Her heart stopped. I'm getting flaky! Here I am, talking to flowers.

She paid for Gram's food, then for her own mints and tiger lily. She kept the two tapes separate. Gram would check prices, that was for sure. And Gram must not know what the tiger lilies cost.

They were a gift.

Mary walked home slowly, guarding the blooms against gusts of wind.

Gram was in the kitchen, sitting at the table. Her fingers were hooked in the handle of a clean cup. Did she want coffee? Had she forgotten to pour it?

Her mind is on Grandpa, I guess. I'm glad I brought her a present. Pleased with herself, Mary thumped down the plant, with its prettiest side facing Gram.

"What's that?" Gram sounded angry.

Was this a mistake? Mary felt shaky.

"Speak up." The old lady was cross.

"Why, it's flowers. Something special, just for you."

"For me?" Gram gently touched one red-orange petal, then another. Her face went soft with a dreamy happiness.

Quietly she said, "Thank you, Betty Sue."

Betty Sue!

Mary's money was spent, and her mother got the credit.

I can't stand it.

"I'm going upstairs to wash my hair," she said.

Giant rollers. A long bath. Three coats of nail polish. Face goop.

All for Ken.

She was starving, but she skipped lunch. She needed to keep distance between herself and Gram.

13

"HEY, Gram! May I borrow a bathrobe or something?" Mary hollered as she rushed downstairs. "Gram, I need something to wear while I iron this dumb dress."

Gram called from the living room, "Come see the flowers."

She likes them! Oh, I'm glad I bought them! Mary's feet were light. She felt like bouncing cloud to cloud.

It always was a shock to come upon Gram suddenly. She was so frail, not at all as Mary remembered her.

This afternoon she sat tightly against a corner of the sofa. There was room enough for another person on the same cushion.

Gram was smiling.

She had cleared the coffee table of its normal litter—an empty candy dish, newspapers, old birthday cards. Only one item remained.

It was the vase Gram liked so much, a tall

blue vase that looked like marble.

In the vase were three flowers.

Tiger lilies.

She's cut them! Oh, she's ruined them! Mary's gasp ended in a sob.

"Didn't I fix them pretty?" Gram asked.

"They're going to die now." Mary felt as if her flesh were frozen.

Gram gazed at her with cloudy, puzzled eyes. The wrinkles in her forehead deepened.

"Is something the matter?" she asked meekly.

Is something the matter? Dear God, everything's the matter! Tears burned like acid in Mary's throat. Her eyesight blurred.

Gram, what has happened to you?

Gram knew the difference between houseplants and the kind of garden flowers that are cut for bouquets.

At least, she used to know the difference.

"The bouquet looks nice," Mary forced herself to say. She bolted upstairs faster than she had come down. She threw herself across her bed and wept. Gram! Gram!

Now there were fresh, deep wrinkles in her dress. She ironed them away. If only troubles could iron away so easily!

The waiting for Ken seemed to stretch forever. Mary spent much of the time fixing her face, repairing telltale trails of tears.

Before five o'clock, she went out to the porch to wait. She took a magazine with her, but she couldn't read. She was too excited.

At the first sight of Ken's blue and green car, she raced to the curb.

He stopped the car where she waited.

She cried, "Oh, those beautiful footlockers!"

But she wasn't looking at her glossy luggage. She was looking at Ken.

He was handsome.

Even in worn, faded clothes, he was handsome.

Mary felt warm joy, like sun at the beach.

Ken unloaded the first footlocker.

Mary grabbed a handle.

With the heavy footlocker between them, they plodded up the path side by side.

Side by side.

It was almost as good as holding hands.

14

THEY made three trips, stacking the footlockers on the porch.

"Well, now we'll take them to your room," Ken said.

"No!"

Oh, why hadn't she guessed this would happen? Now, she had to keep him out of her room. It was the pits. The bed wasn't made. Hair rollers were wherever they had landed—on the dresser, on the floor, on the bed. Makeup was spread around. The yearbook from California, the address book, the autograph book . . . All scattered. Nothing neat.

No, he couldn't see that room!

She said, "Boys aren't allowed upstairs. Gram is old-fashioned, you know." Please, God, don't let her say something to peg me a liar.

"So I'm not trusted?" He laughed. "Well, that's good for my ego."

Weak with relief, she sank into the swing.

The chains moaned.

"Laugh all you want," she said. "But you wouldn't laugh if you had to live here."

He sat beside her.

The swing was perfect for two people. Her hip touched his.

She told him about the cut tiger lilies.

"She keeps me uptight," she complained. "I never know what she'll do next."

"You'll get used to her ways," Ken said.

What if I don't want to? What if I want to live my senior year someplace where there are no worries and no surprises?

She wailed, "Let me tell you what Olga wants me to do. She wants me to wait till Gram is asleep, then sneak away her underwear. Otherwise she keeps wearing the same dirty stuff."

Her cheeks burned hot. This was too personal to talk about, but Ken was a good listener. If she didn't confide in somebody, she would explode.

Ken said, "You should be able to manage the underwear."

"Why should I?" She choked on a sob. "It's— it's gross."

"Someday you, too, will grow old."

"Don't remind me! It's horrible!"

"It's not horrible at all. It's part of life."

"It's easy enough for you to talk!" Mary cried. "She's not your grandmother."

75

"If she were, I'd try—"

Anger pounded at Mary. "You don't think I try! That's not fair!" She jumped from the swing, choking out, "I think she's crazy!"

He followed her, and the swing shuddered to a halt.

"You don't mean that," he said.

"I do mean it! I do!"

Her fist pressed against her mouth. Horror flashed like disco lights. Gram, I don't mean it!

Ken said, "You're carrying a load of anger, aren't you?"

"Isn't that my right?" she blasted.

"You have the right to do anything you please, as far as I'm concerned." His voice was cold.

He walked around the footlockers and started down the steps.

"Wait!" she cried. "Can't you stay to dinner? We've got some spaghetti in a can—"

"Another time." His tone of voice said clearly, There won't be another time.

He got into his car and drove away.

She watched the empty street long, long after he was gone. Oh, why couldn't he understand how rough it was to live with Gram? Why couldn't he give some sympathy?

15

"OH, Betty Sue, there you are." Gram joined Mary on the porch.

She was clutching her purse tightly against her chest. Her wig was atilt.

"I'm going to the store," she announced.

Her frail shoulders sagged more than usual. Her face drooped in tired lines. Toward night, she always wore down.

Mary doubted that Gram had the energy to shop. But how could she stop the old lady? Gram didn't welcome advice.

She tried, "Listen, Gram, the stores will close soon. Let's save our errands till tomorrow."

"You forgot to buy a can of tuna," Gram whined.

"I did?" News to me.

"I had it on the list."

You did not!

Mary knew better than to argue. Once Gram fixed an idea in her mind, it was there to stay.

"I always keep tuna on hand." Gram's voice was firm.

Mary reminded her, "We're having spaghetti tonight. I'll buy the tuna tomorrow."

"It's for company," Gram said.

"Are we having company?"

"Somebody might drop in."

But nobody visited Gram anymore. Olga had said so, and it made Mary sad. Gram's lifelong friends had died or moved away, or were too sick to call.

Mary spoke over the lump in her throat. "Since you really need the tuna, Gram, I'll go get it." She held out her hand as if expecting the car keys. Maybe this time . . .

It didn't work.

Gram said in a huff, "I'm going to the store, and I'm going alone." Carelessly, too quickly, she flitted down the steps.

Mary held her breath. Gram was like a blown-glass figure, too fragile even to touch.

Still at a pell-mell pace, the old lady crossed the grass to her car.

Even her shadow looked breakable, Mary thought.

Gram backed out of the driveway in frantic haste.

Dear God, take care of her!

Mary had a fleeting thought: I should have straightened her wig.

She was too jittery to wait for Gram on the porch, so she unloaded her footlockers, carrying her belongings by armloads up to her room. While she worked, she played her tapes.

Loudly.

Sound was alive in the room.

Mary sang along, "I talked too fast, I talked too foolish, I lost my one true love."

Gravel collected in Mary's throat. The song was so sad! It was like her scene with Ken, out on the porch.

The telephone rang.

"Ken!"

She had been thinking of him. He had been thinking of her.

She said, "Hello," with joy in her heart.

The answering voice was female.

Oh, darn.

Half deaf with disappointment, Mary waited.

"I am calling from Lost Creek Hospital."

Hospital! Frightened, Mary pressed the receiver tighter against her ear.

The voice was brisk, almost like a recording. "We have admitted a Mrs. Kornman—"

"Gram!" Mary cried. "She crashed her car!"

"It wasn't an auto accident."

"What happened, then?" Mary was trembling.

"She fell. In a shopping center, I believe. She is asking for Doctor Jasper, and we have sent for him."

"Yes." Mary's jaw felt stiff. "Thanks for calling."

She stared at the phone long after the call ended. Nerves pinched her stomach. Hammers pounded her head.

Gram, oh, Gram! Don't be sick.

Don't be hurt.

Oh, please don't die!

She put her fingers against her cheeks and whispered, "Gram, I love you."

16

GRAM'S room at the hospital was a double one with a screen between the two beds.

Moans came from behind the screen.

Gram didn't moan. She lay silently in the bed nearer the door.

Her small body hardly made a bump under the covers. Her face was gray against the white pillowcase. The wig was gone.

When she saw Mary, she lifted herself from her pillow. "Promise me," she begged. "Promise you'll never put me in a nursing home."

How can I promise that?

Mary wanted to run away. Instead she gasped in gulps of too-clean hospital air. It reeked of chemicals and made her nose tickle.

"Rest, now." Mary eased the old shoulders back onto the pillow.

"Thank you, Betty Sue."

Mom always got the credit . . .

No matter. This wasn't a time for hurt feelings. What mattered was Gram.

And Mary's duty toward Gram.

What was she supposed to do? Where could she turn for help?

Gram gazed at Mary from the depths of her pillow.

"Close your eyes now," Mary soothed.

Gram obeyed.

Mary held Gram's hand. It was a bunch of brittle bones. Its strength was gone.

In tears, Mary remembered the magic spun by those hands—the miracles that came from the oven, and the hard and joyful hugs that set the world right.

Now it was Mary's turn to spin magic, to return favors.

She didn't know how.

And she felt guilty.

A doctor walked into the room and called Gram by name.

Mary went to wait in the hall.

Far down the hall, a nurse in white hurried on silent feet to answer a light. A red-haired man in a wheelchair made a U-turn and headed back Mary's way.

He zoomed toward her as if demons followed.

She moved close to the wall, to give him plenty of racetrack.

He slowed as he passed her.

"Ankle broken in three places," he reported, as if Mary had asked.

Before she could reply, he picked up speed and was gone.

At the other end of the hall, he U-turned again and came back.

"Guys in wheelchairs even play basketball," he said as he passed.

Again she had no chance to reply.

Next time I'll speak first, she decided.

But he disappeared into a room.

It seemed forever before Gram's doctor came into the hall.

He was a dark man with bushy black eyebrows and a hawk nose. He carried a folder.

He seemed deep in thought and didn't notice Mary.

As he started down the hall, she kept pace beside him. "Tell me!" she begged. "How is she?"

He seemed to see her for the first time.

"I'm asking about Mrs. Kornman," Mary said. "How is she?"

"We'll let her rest now," the doctor said.

Why didn't he answer her question? Were things really bad? Problems pounded at Mary. What am I supposed to do now? Where do I go from here?

The doctor went on down the hall.

Mary grabbed his elbow. "I've got to know

what to expect. I've got to know what to do."

He eyed her coldly. "That I'll discuss with her daughter."

"Her daughter is in South America," Mary said.

"On the contrary. She's living with Mrs. Kornman right now."

"No, she isn't. It's me! I live with her. I'm her granddaughter."

Still the doctor seemed doubtful.

Mary was forced to admit, "She mixes us up, sometimes."

"I see."

Suddenly he seemed to see a great deal, to see things Mary herself didn't see. For the first time, he looked at Mary as if she were important, as if she mattered.

He led her past the nurses' station to a small lobby. There was a table with magazines, a huge coffeepot, and six chairs.

"Sit." He sounded like a man who always was obeyed.

Mary sat.

He poured coffee for himself and Mary.

Usually she drank coffee only with milk and three spoons of sugar. But the doctor gave her no choice, and she was asking no favors.

Dutifully she sipped.

The brew was bitter.

84

It went straight to the achy place in her throat where tears were piling up.

With his coffee in his big hand, the man sat opposite Mary. His eyes were shadowed. His shoulders slumped. He looked very tired.

Mary remembered he had been called to the hospital from his home. This was the dinner hour. No doubt he was hungry as well as tired.

She wasn't hungry. Her stomach was too knotted.

17

MARY told her name. Dr. Jasper told his.

He judged her. "So, Miss Mary Glass, you are finding life with your grandmother difficult?"

She squirmed. He was too good at reading her mind.

She tried to explain. "Gram's so changed. She used to be peppy. Organized. Fun to be with. Now she's all mixed up. She hides things and can't find them. She can't remember what happened yesterday."

"But she remembers what happened fifty years ago, and twenty-five . . ."

Mary's eyes widened. "How did you know?"

"It's all part of the pattern."

"What pattern?" Mary grasped at the clue like a drowning person grasping a lifeline.

Instead of answering, he poured himself another cup of coffee.

Mary told his back, "Guess what she said to me? When I got here to the hospital? The first thing she said was, 'Promise you won't put me in a nursing home.' "

The doctor came back to his seat. He leaned forward. His dark eyes met Mary's. "People like your grandmother do better in their own homes. Where they know their way around. Where there are familiar things to touch, to bring back memories."

She pounced on his first words. "Dr. Jasper, what do you mean by 'people like my grandmother'?"

He studied her.

She felt like a pinup bug in a science class.

In time he asked, "Is anybody else in your house? Or is it just you and your grandmother?"

"Once a week, Olga comes to clean. She has come every Thursday for years. She's one of the family, almost."

"I see."

What did he see? She, for one, wasn't learning much.

Dr. Jasper said, "You must remember your grandmother is getting older."

"So is Olga! She's crippled, but her mind is sharp. She's not—" Mary gasped a breath. Could she voice the cruel word? The cruel but fitting word?

She choked out, "Olga's not flaky."

Flaky. What an ugly thing to say about Gram!

Mary touched clammy hands to hot cheeks.

Dr. Jasper said, "People age in different ways. As you know, some old folks are hard-of-hearing and some are not. Some have failing eyesight. Some do not. Gray hair and wrinkled skin come early or late.

"It's the same with memory. It can hold firm or it can fail."

"Poor Gram," Mary said.

"Let's not deal in pity." He frowned, and his eyebrows met above his hawk nose. "Mary, there is no rule that says memory problems must go on. A healthy person keeps a sharp mind all through life."

He went on. "Your grandmother suffered a shock—her husband died."

"That was a year ago."

"Remember, she took care of him for fifty years. She misses him. No wonder it is hard for her to think straight."

"She pretends he's alive. Maybe she believes it. She keeps saying he'll fix the drippy faucet—"

"I suggest you learn to fix the faucet." He was stern.

"Well, it's hard to do anything. Gram's so up-tight about money. She's scared she's being cheated."

The doctor didn't seem surprised.

Mary wailed, "I'm not used to it! I don't think

she trusts even me. She made a big point of showing me where she hid emergency dollars. They were stitched into the hem of a curtain.

"So I was going to use that money for a cab to the hospital, but it was gone."

Dr. Jasper said, "She moved her money to a different hiding place. The elderly often do this."

"It bugs me!"

"Well, sure." For a moment, he sounded human.

Mary went on, "She tells the same stories over and over."

"It is her way to gain attention. To be noticed."

"But it's the same stuff, over and over."

"Maybe it is hard for her to form new ideas. There is some safety in keeping to the same groove. By the way, does she hear voices?"

"Voices?" Mary echoed.

"Voices that give her orders—tell her to do this or that?"

Mary was glad she could answer no.

"How about wandering?" the doctor asked. "Does she leave the house, walk around the neighborhood?"

"Not that I know. I'll ask Olga."

"Some elderly people walk and walk. It eases stress. But often their families think they are running away."

89

Mary pictured Gram out in the road, walking, while cars whizzed past her. Fear squeezed tightly.

She choked out, "Oh, Dr. Jasper, I can't lock Gram inside the house!"

"It is not my idea to turn you into a policeman. It is not my idea to place your grandmother in any danger. But I do feel she can go on living in her own home—with your help, maybe. Meanwhile I am going to order a complete medical work-up."

"What's that?"

"Tests. We will run them while she is here in the hospital. We will try to find the cause of her problems."

Mary felt sad. "Gram's so old."

"Don't harp on her age!" The doctor's words were knives. "Many medical conditions can make a person forgetful. A head injury, for example. An infection. A faulty diet. Anemia. Thyroid problems. Pressure on nerves. A tumor in the skull. The wrong drugs, or drugs in the wrong combination."

"She takes pills, but sometimes she forgets, I think," Mary reported.

"You might make a chart for her, or dole out the pills as needed."

How easy he made it sound!

Mary said, "But Dr. Jasper, Gram won't listen to me. I can't even keep her out of the car, and she's going to kill herself in that car!"

"We'll test her eyes, of course. And her hearing. And her reflexes. If there is any medical reason she should not drive, I will ask that she quit."

"Thank you!" For the first time, it seemed, the doctor was on Mary's side.

So she asked him, "Will you write to my parents? To tell them what's the matter with Gram?"

"What we do in these cases is write a brief report. If your parents need more information, they can telephone to me."

He's not going to put much into writing, Mary saw. Yet this was a start.

Perhaps Dr. Jasper sensed her worry. He promised, "I won't ask too much of you."

"If I stick around, I might need help," she warned.

"I'm here to help."

He meant it! She whispered, "Thanks."

He said, "Let's see. This is Friday. The lab will begin tests on Monday."

Not until Monday. Monday seemed a year away.

Mary asked, "When can Gram come home?" Suddenly the house on Elm Street seemed like home.

The doctor stalled. "She had a fall, you know. Sometimes problems show up later. We will watch her."

"Watch her?" Mary echoed.

"Well, she will be right here under our noses, right here in the hospital. Her tests won't be finished until Wednesday or Thursday."

Such a long time.

Mary returned to Gram's room.

Gram was sleeping.

Mary waited.

Much of her fear was gone. Her burden seemed lighter.

Dr. Jasper would help her when she needed help.

18

BACK in the house on Elm Street, Mary missed Gram. She was surprised.

When she went to bed, the old house began talking. Air seeped through cracks, whispering. Old boards groaned. Ghosts floated.

Mary lay on her back, her hands gripping the top sheet. She swallowed and swallowed, but the bitter taste of fear kept coming back.

Grow up! she scolded herself.

But the old house played joke after noisy joke on her.

Think about something else!

She planned the next day.

When the next day came, the plan seemed foolish. Ken would see right through her, that was for sure!

But what else could she do? She didn't know anybody else except Olga.

Her hike to the depot was familiar now, past yards with flowers, then through the seedy downtown. All the downtown stores looked faded and tired. The bright new stores were built at the edge of town.

Mary stood in front of Jake's Pawn Shop and looked across the street to the bus depot. Did she dare? Ken had been mad when he left her. He might not want to see her again.

I'll just ask my one favor, and then I'll get out of there.

Ken was not in the depot. An elderly man stood behind the ticket window.

"Where's Ken Clayton?" Mary blurted.

"He's off weekends."

"Oh!"

Of course Ken wouldn't work seven days a week.

She trudged home. There she telephoned Ken before she lost courage. "I don't want to be a pest," she told him, "but I need help."

"Be right over," he promised.

Her thanks came from deep in her soul.

She zoomed through the downstairs, picking up everything that was out of place. Today she could invite him inside.

She led him to the living room. How formal they acted! They faced each other across the tiger lilies.

He was wearing the same frayed shirt he had worn the day they met. Mary hoped that was a good sign. Maybe they could start over again, from the beginning.

In a rush, she said, "Ken, I know you're mad at me, but I need help. Gram still won't let me drive. She said I had to find an adult."

She made a face. She felt very adult. In fact, with her new duties, she felt a hundred years old.

In a flood of words, she told about Gram's accident.

She told other things she had kept secret before. They were truths that tore her heart.

When she ended, Ken said softly, "You have to face it. Your grandmother is senile."

"Don't say that! Dr. Jasper said never to use that word!"

"Words don't change facts."

"Well, smarty, you've got your facts screwed up." Her pulses pounded. There they went again, at each other's throats.

"Your grandmother is mixed up," Ken pointed out. "You said so yourself. You called her flaky."

Shame burned inside her. She said, "That was tacky of me. I just didn't understand. Gram is sick, you know, but she can get better. Dr. Jasper is going to help her." Mary had faith.

Ken insisted, "Old folks get senile."

"Not all old folks! Only five or six percent of them. They get something called senile dementia, and it can't be cured." She gasped a breath. "But Gram's not one of that five or six percent! The tests will prove that."

She crossed her fingers for luck. The tests had to turn out well, they just had to! Gram had to be O.K.

Ken argued, "Old folks' arteries clog up, like bubble gum in a garden hose. So not enough blood gets to the brain to feed it. Then people get flaky. I think it's called hardening of the arteries."

"You ought to talk to Dr. Jasper."

Ken spoke gently, "Aw, Mary, I've known lots of old folks, and they're all the same."

"No, they're not! Most of them just need different medicine or tender loving care."

"Have it your way." Clearly, he had not changed his mind.

She kept on. "Listen, if you lose your car keys, nobody thinks much about it. If you forget somebody's name, you shrug it off. But if an old person loses keys or forgets a name, we think right away, senile."

"You've got a point," he said.

With a lump in her throat, she added, "Gram's so cute sometimes, I could hug her to pieces. Other times, she drives me batty."

Ken said, "That sounds like any two people living together."

"It does?"

"Well, it sounds like Mom and me."

Mary felt lonely for her own mother and the quarrels they had. But today was today, with its own problems. She asked, "Ken, will you get Gram's car?"

"If I drive hers home, you'll have to drive mine."

Her heart leaped. At last she would get her hands on a steering wheel!

"I'm all out of practice," she said.

"Then drive over to the shopping center. I'll sit beside you in case you need help."

"Backseat driving from the front seat." Her grumpy tone hid her joy. To drive would be great.

But what really mattered was that Ken trusted her.

19

MARY spent a lot of time with Gram in the hospital. They didn't talk much. But Gram seemed happy Mary was there.

Gram's car keys were in Mary's purse, but she didn't sneak even a tiny ride. She wanted to prove to herself that she was "adult." If she knew it deep inside herself, Gram would know it, too.

Thursday was the day set for Gram to come home.

Olga and Mary worked together to get the house ready. There wasn't much litter to pick up. All week, Mary had worked at keeping things neat. She didn't want Ken to know she was a slob.

Maybe she wasn't a slob. Picking up was becoming a habit.

Olga threw out the tiger lilies. They were dead.

A little after five o'clock, Ken drove up in his wreck of a car.

They would bring Gram home in her own Dodge. To get into Ken's car, the passenger had to slide under the steering wheel. Gram wasn't up to that.

Ken opened the Dodge door for Mary. He said, "You're wearing the dress I like."

That's why I wore it.

"You look good in yellow," he added.

"I look good in jeans." Grinning, she admitted, "Even jeans get boring."

The car door slammed.

Ken revved the motor. "Well, let's go get your grandmother out of hock."

"Hock is right." Mary laughed. "Good thing she has Medicare and stuff like that."

"Good thing she has you," Ken said.

"Isn't that the truth?" Mary spoke lightly. Since Gram's accident, she had begun to feel different about the trap she was in.

She tried to explain as Ken drove. "I always thought my senior year in high school would be the best year of my life."

"Maybe it will be."

She looked sideways at him. With him in the picture, yes, maybe it would be the best year of her whole life.

She wondered about his life before they met. "Ken, did you have fun your senior year?"

"I was too busy working nights to notice."

"That's awful. I'm sorry you had to work so hard."

"Don't be sorry. I like to work."

Her eyes misted. "It'll pay off for you, Ken, I know it will! You'll have your own plumbing business and . . ."

And maybe there'll be a place in your life for me.

It was funny the way things worked out, she thought. First she had missed her parents' telephone call. Then they missed her return call. When she cried out her heart in a letter, it sounded babyish and petty, and she had never mailed it.

So what had seemed setbacks turned out to be gifts of time. Time to understand what was what. Time to screw her head on straight.

All her life, people had taken care of her. Now it was her turn to take care of somebody.

She told Ken, "I really don't miss the hustle and bustle of L.A. too much."

His right hand left the steering wheel and gripped hers.

She felt the jolt of his touch clear to her toes.

She never had felt that way about Johnny Bryan.

With a small wobble in her voice, she said, "You know, being without friends here in Lost Creek made me understand Gram better. All her friends are gone. It's real sad."

"You'll make lots of friends here," Ken promised.

She smiled a secret smile. With luck, Ken would stay her very best friend. She wanted to be his girl.

She said, "Ken, you'll never believe this, but I'm going to learn to cook."

"Orders from your stomach?"

"Orders from Dr. Jasper. Gram needs a balanced diet. And you're right. I'm sick of meals out of cans."

"Don't burn the house down," he warned.

Did he have to turn everything into a joke? Well, she wouldn't tell him Dr. Jasper's other orders for Gram's welfare.

She was going to make Gram feel important. She was going to keep her busy. Whenever one of Gram's projects turned out right, she was going to praise her and praise her. She would make Gram feel useful and needed. If Gram goofed, well, that could be passed over lightly. Gram mustn't brood about what might have been.

The most important thing, Dr. Jasper said, was to let Gram know she was loved.

Ken pulled into the hospital parking lot.

"I'll go get her," Mary said. "You wait here. O.K?"

"O.K."

Gram was sitting in the chair in her room,

dressed, her wig in place. A nurse had fixed her up, no doubt.

She looked darling. She almost looked young.

From behind the screen, Gram's roommate moaned.

Mary said, "Gram, it's time to go home."

A shadow crossed the old woman's face. "The doctor said tomorrow."

"That's exactly what he said," Mary agreed. "He said that yesterday."

"Was that yesterday?" Gram seemed surprised. "What happened to yesterday?"

What happened to yesterday?

Tears gathered in Mary's throat. She swallowed them away. No longer would she cry about things like that.

"Oh, Gram, don't worry about yesterday." She helped the old lady stand up. "Let's just think about today."

She hugged Gram, hugged her hard.

Gram hugged back with all her strength and joy.

Together they left the hospital. At the foot of the steps Ken was waiting. To see him there was as good as feeling Gram's hug.

"Ken, here we are!" Mary called happily. "We're coming home."

About the Author

DOROTHY KAYSER FRENCH's writing career began at the age of eleven when *The Milwaukee Journal* printed her letter to the editor. From that point, she was hooked on seeing her words in print. She wrote for school publications in grade school, high school, and college.

After graduation from the journalism school of the University of Wisconsin-Madison, she worked for newspapers in Wisconsin and Oklahoma. More than two hundred of her short stories and articles have been published in American and British magazines, and her many books have been written for children of all ages.

She is the wife of Louis N. French, associate patent counsel for Phillips Petroleum Company. The Frenches have two daughters, and part of her writing efforts kept pace with her daughters' growth. Now the cycle is beginning again; she is writing for three young grandsons.

DISCARD

DATE DUE

NOV 3 '82			
APR 25 '86			
SEP 2 1 1991			
GAYLORD			PRINTED IN U.S.A.